Zia

Loud, confident and intrepid. She's a born leader but can sometimes get carried away. Likes schoolwork and wants to be a scientist when she's older, just like her mum.

Thunder

Big, white and fluffy with grey ears, paws and tail. He's blind in one eye, but that's what makes him extra special. Likes chasing mice, climbing trees and going on adventures. Is also a cat.

Join Katy, Cassie and Zia
on more Playdate Adventures

The Wishing Star
The North Pole Picnic
The Giant Conker

THE MAGIC OCEAN SLIDE

THE PLAYDATE
ADVENTURES

Book Three

THE MAGIC
OCEAN
SLIDE

Emma Beswetherick

Illustrated by Anna Woodbine

ROCK THE BOAT

A Rock the Boat Book

First published by Rock the Boat,
an imprint of Oneworld Publications, 2021

Text copyright © Emma Beswetherick, 2021
Illustration copyright © The Woodbine Workshop, 2021

The moral right of Emma Beswetherick and the Woodbine Workshop
to be identified as the Author and Illustrator of this work respectively has
been asserted by them in accordance with the Copyright, Designs, and
Patents Act 1988

ISBN 978-1-78607-898-8 (paperback)
ISBN 978-1-78607-899-5 (ebook)

Printed and bound in Great Britain by Clays Ltd, Elcograf S.p.A.

This book is a work of fiction. Names, characters, businesses, organisations,
places and events are either the product of the author's imagination or are used
fictitiously. Any resemblance to actual persons, living or dead, events
or locales is entirely coincidental.

Oneworld Publications
10 Bloomsbury Street, London, WC1B 3SR, England

Stay up to date with the latest books,
special offers, and exclusive content from
Rock the Boat with our newsletter

Sign up on our website
oneworld-publications.com/rtb

To Tony, Archie and Isla,
for the fun and laughter we've had at waterparks

CHAPTER ONE

It was the hottest day of the summer. The country was basking in a heatwave and people everywhere were doing whatever they could to stay cool – which, for Katy, involved sitting in her messy bedroom, window wide open, ice lolly in hand.

It should have been the perfect way to spend her afternoon after a long, baking hot day at school. But Katy was feeling fed up. She was supposed to be on a playdate at Cassandra's house with their friend Zia. But Cassandra's

1

brother had chickenpox and, as it was almost the school holidays, Katy wasn't allowed to visit in case she got chickenpox too. That meant the playdate had been cancelled. That was the reason Katy was feeling sad.

The thing was, Katy had been dying to go on a playdate today. She'd been dreaming about it for weeks and weeks. Not only was she in the same class as Zia and Cassandra at school, they were also in a secret club called the Playdate Adventure Club. Nobody – not their parents, their teachers nor the other children in their class – knew anything about the magical adventures they got up to on their playdates. Now it had been cancelled, there was no chance of them having another adventure today.

Katy sighed as she flopped onto her unmade bed, stroking her cat Thunder's fluffy white tummy. He was sprawled on his back, looking very much like the other plump cushions scattered around her pillow. Even with her window open and a fan blowing full blast in her room, she felt sticky and uncomfortable. It looked like Thunder did too. Today definitely wasn't a very good day.

Then: "Katy! Come here! I've got something to tell you!" her dad shouted from across the landing.

Katy stopped stroking Thunder and moped her way into the kitchen, Thunder trotting lazily behind.

"What is it, Dad?" she asked sullenly.

"Do you want cheering up?"

"Well, duh!" she said, dropping her lolly stick into the bin.

"I just got off the phone to Cassie's mum," he said, a wide smile on his face.  "Cassie's already had chickenpox so won't be contagious. She and Zia are on their way here for a playdate instead. You don't mind, do you?"

"Mind?" Katy squealed, heaving Thunder into her arms and waltzing with him around the kitchen. "That's the best news I've heard all day! Thanks, Dad. Love you," she sang, then charged back into her messy room to get ready for her friends.

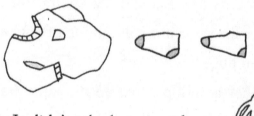

It didn't take long to tidy up. Her room wasn't big and she didn't have a huge selection of toys. She picked up the ones strewn across her carpet and threw them into a toy box in the corner, then put her clothes away in the wardrobe. She was just straightening her duvet when she heard the doorbell.

"I'll get it!" she shouted, bounding down the stairs three at a time in her eagerness to get to the door first. Her dad followed – she wasn't supposed to open the door without supervision.

As she pulled the handle down and the door swung towards her, Zia and Cassandra threw themselves forwards in a commotion of hot air, giggles and hugs.

Then they all ran panting up the stairs and across the landing to Katy's bedroom, with shouts of "Bye, Mum!" and "Don't disturb us, will you, Dad?" and "See you later!" before Katy closed the door behind them.

"I'm glad you're here," Katy said when they were finally alone. "I've been miserable since our playdate was cancelled!"

"Me too," agreed Zia, wiping her brow.

"And me," said Cassandra. "I've waited ages to have you two over to my house. I can't believe my baby brother chose today to go and get chickenpox!"

"At least your dad said we could come here again." Zia smiled at Katy. They'd last been in Katy's room during their first ever playdate together. Then, they'd made a space rocket out of cardboard boxes and bits of junk, which had magically turned into an actual spaceship and taken them on an adventure to the stars. Katy had been wondering all week if something just as incredible was going to happen during their playdate today. Now they were all together, she finally dared to imagine it might.

"It's so hot!" whined Cassandra, fanning her face where drops of sweat were shining off her freckles. She was wearing even more hair clips than usual to keep her Afro away from her sweaty face.

7

"Mum says she doesn't even remember feeling this hot when she grew up in India!" Zia sighed, holding her long plait away from her neck to cool herself down.

"Really?" said Katy. "That's crazy!"

Zia nodded. "I wish we had a swimming pool."

"Sorry, but I don't even have a paddling pool." Katy lived with her dad and Thunder on the upstairs floor of a two-storey townhouse. She loved living here, but right now, when it was so hot in her room, she'd give anything to have a garden to play in – and a paddling pool to cool down in. "Tell us what you had planned for us, Cassie. I like Zia's idea – please say it involves jumping into water."

Cassandra smiled, her dark, mischievous eyes lighting up the bedroom. "It does involve getting wet!"

"Is it to the beach?" said Zia eagerly.

"Or perhaps the ocean?" Katy asked.

They'd been learning about the ocean that term at school and Katy had found it really interesting, especially when their teacher, Ms Coco, had taught them about all the different creatures that lived underwater.

"Bingo!" said Cassandra, spinning around in one of her legendary street dance moves. "I thought we could go on an ocean adventure. What do you think?"

"I think that's the best idea!" Zia jumped up from the bed with excitement.

"I agree," said Katy happily, glad her friend had come armed with such an awesome plan. "Have you worked out how we're going to get there?"

"I have!" said Cassie, smiling. "And you're going to love it. All we need is a slide…"

CHAPTER TWO

"A slide?" asked Zia.

Cassandra strolled over to the window and gazed out into the hazy sunshine.

"If we'd been at my house, we'd have started our adventure outside in the paddling pool. But now we're here, I think a waterslide out of Katy's bedroom window, straight into the ocean, would be kind of cool."

Katy clapped her hands together. "I've always wondered what that would be like! Could it be like those flumes you get at water parks – the ones that loop around and around as you rush down into the water?"

"And it could have big drops and whirlpools and jets of water that shoot out at you as you go down!" Zia's almond-shaped eyes sparkled enthusiastically.

"Yes – all of those," said Cassandra. "But rather than dropping us into a swimming pool, it takes us straight into the ocean!"

"Brilliant! Let's draw it!" Katy felt excited already and they hadn't even begun their adventure. She started rummaging through her cupboard to find her art and craft box, just as Thunder trotted over and started nudging his head against her knees.

"Thunder, not now," she said, as she pulled out her drawing pad and pencil case. Again, Thunder butted his head against her legs, a worried look on his face. "What is it?" she asked, knowing full well her cat couldn't tell her what he was really thinking.

"Perhaps it has something to do with our adventure?" Zia suggested.

"You could be right," said Katy, putting down her pencil case and swapping it for a miserable-looking Thunder. "Don't you like the sound of an ocean adventure?" she said, cradling his fluffy white body in her arms and kissing him on the top of his furry grey head. "I know you hate getting wet, but I'm sure you're going to enjoy it."

Thunder meowed and looked up at her with his one big, blue eye. He'd lost the other one in a fight when he was a kitten. Katy's dad said it was what made him extra special.

"That's what it is," she said to her friends. "I'm sure of it. Cats hate water. What should we do?"

They all thought for a moment.

"Perhaps we need our adventure to give us magical powers," said Cassandra.

"Powers that turn even the most water-hating animal into a water-loving one?" Katy giggled.

"Exactly," said Cassandra.

"And how about special underwater breathing powers?" Zia suggested. "It would be really cool if we could dive deep down in the ocean without needing oxygen tanks!" Zia wanted to be a scientist when she grew up, just like her mum, and always came up with the most scientific ideas.

"I was just thinking that," said Cassandra. "If we're having an adventure in the ocean, we need to be able to swim under the water as well as through it. Otherwise, we won't really be having an adventure at all."

Katy grabbed her pad of paper and started scribbling a diagram of the waterslide. She loved drawing and her dad said she was really good. The sketch had loop the loops and big drops and whirlpools and jets of water, just as they'd discussed.

"What else should it have?" Katy asked. "Remember, this can be the craziest slide in the history of the world!"

"Let's add a lazy river," said Cassandra dreamily. "I went on this amazing one last year with my family. It wound itself around the water park, in and out of all the slides. Everyone sat in big rings shaped like doughnuts and the river pulled you along in a really strong current. Sometimes a huge wave would come and push you even faster." She chuckled, remembering. "I loved it so much!"

Of the three friends, Zia was usually the bravest and Cassandra the most cautious when it came to adventures. But swimming was one of Cassandra's favourite hobbies, so this adventure was right up her street.

Katy was deep in concentration, scribbling away. Then: "Something like this?" she said when she'd finished.

"Exactly like that!" said Cassandra, smiling.

But Zia was still staring at the drawing, one finger pressed to her lips as her brain went into overdrive. "I think it needs two more things," she blurted out. "Let's add flashing lights and music. If this is going to be the coolest slide in the history of the world, surely we can have a disco on our way down as well!"

"Yes!" shouted Cassandra. "Then I can practise my two favourite things at the same time – swimming and street dance!" She spun round in a circle and punched the air with her fist.

They all laughed.

Katy was amazed by Cassandra's enthusiasm today. On previous playdates, Katy and Zia had had to help their friend overcome her nervousness, otherwise she might not have had the courage to join them on their adventures at all. But today she seemed so much more confident.

"OK, who's ready to go on an adventure?" said Zia. She wasn't always the best at being patient, but only because she got so carried away by the games they played.

They all knew the drill by now. They'd been on enough adventures to know what to do.

They formed a tight circle and held hands with their eyes closed, Thunder in the middle.

"Over to you, Cassie," said Katy encouragingly, eyes squeezed tightly shut.

Cassandra took a deep breath in. "I want you to imagine an enormous, magical slide coming out of Katy's bedroom window, with a lazy river winding around it, just like in the picture – but even cooler, if that's possible, and more magical. One that twists and turns and drops us into the middle of the ocean. Now repeat after me: I wish to go on an adventure."

"*I wish to go on an adventure,*" the girls sang in unison.

Immediately, electricity started shooting around their bodies. It was like electricity anyway – they felt kind of hot and cold and fizzy and bubbly all at the same time, as though they had become super-charged with superpowers. It only took a few seconds for the sensation to fade away.

Then they slowly opened their eyes.

CHAPTER THREE

"OH…" cried Cassandra.

"MY…" squealed Zia.

"GOODNESS!" shrieked Katy.

Spiralling from the window and out across the rooftops was the most incredible waterslide they had ever seen. The inside of the tube was big enough for the girls to step into easily without getting squashed. They peered through the entrance and saw there were jets shooting water in a fast stream down the middle. When they looked down at themselves, they also saw that instead of their school uniforms, they were now wearing brightly coloured swimsuits, including Thunder, who still looked cross – but perhaps not quite as cross as he did before.

"Are you ready?" asked Cassandra. "Katy, this is your playdate, so do you want to go first?"

"No, you go," Katy replied. "I know it's my house, but it's your adventure."

"If you're sure?" said Cassandra, looking at her friends gratefully. "Zia, ready?" she asked, knowing, of course, that she would be.

"Ready!" cried Zia, with an enthusiastic smile. "Katy, you go second – so I can pass you Thunder."

"Good idea." Katy smiled. "Thanks, Zia."

"OK, let's go!" Cassandra climbed carefully onto Katy's windowsill and sat on the edge with her legs stretched out in front, looking down at the drop below.

"Cassie, are you OK?" Katy asked.

"Er, I thought I was, but now I'm not so sure," Cassandra replied nervously.

Katy placed one hand comfortingly on her friend's shoulder. "I know it seems crazy to jump out of the window into the unknown," she said kindly. "But we're the Playdate Adventure Club and this is YOUR magical adventure."

"And we're right behind you, Cassie," Zia added encouragingly. "We're all in this together, remember?"

Cassandra looked pale as she twisted her head round to look at her friends. "I know you're right. Just give me a moment, OK?"

They waited patiently while Cassandra's gaze turned back towards her toes. They waited, and they waited some more. Then, just as Katy was about to offer some more words of encouragement, Cassandra disappeared with a great big WHOOSH and a shriek of delight. She was off!

Cassandra's nerves were forgotten at once as the excitement of the ride took over. Zooming down the flume, whooshing right, then left, then up, then down, she knew right away that this was her absolute favourite playdate adventure yet. Even cooler than competing in a swimming race in the Arctic! Even cooler than flying in a rocket into space! And to top it off, her favourite pop song was echoing all around her, and there were colourful lights flashing in time to the beat. The flume was dark and scary in places, but also amazing. She was in her very own waterslide disco!

"Thank goodness she did it!" Zia exclaimed, peering down the slide from Katy's bedroom window. "But I hope she's OK. Your turn now, Katy."

Katy's tummy felt full of butterflies as she climbed onto the ledge, holding onto the sides tightly so as not to slip down without her cat. Zia placed Thunder's great, heavy weight on her lap and as soon as Katy let go to put her arms around him, they were off, zooming down so fast Katy almost forgot to breathe.

25

"Thunder – *cough*! – are you – *cough*! – OK?" she spluttered as water shot up through her nostrils. She couldn't hear his reply because her words echoed around the inside of the tube and got lost in the music. She felt the beat pulse through her body and began to sing along at the top of her voice. She would never forget this ride, not in a million years!

Finally, she landed with an enormous splash into a deep pool of water. Her head went under and her whole body felt shocked by the sudden cold. Then she came up spluttering and laughing, together with a coughing and spluttering cat.

"Is everyone OK?" she shouted, when Zia's head popped above the surface a moment later.

"That was brilliant!" shrieked Zia. "I can't believe the slide even played music!"

"It really is the best waterslide ever!" Cassandra laughed, clearing water from her nose.

"I wouldn't say that," moaned Thunder, frantically treading water with his two front paws. During an adventure he always amazed the friends when he started talking like a human – albeit a grumpy one.

"Come on, you know an adventure wouldn't be the same without you," said Katy, drawing him into her arms so he didn't have to paddle so hard. "You'll always be part of the Playdate Adventure Club."

"That doesn't mean I have to like it," he retorted. But then he winked with his one eye and grinned, and Katy knew he was OK.

The girls took some time to look all around them and it soon became clear they weren't in the ocean. The water wasn't salty and there weren't any fish in sight. It felt more like a swimming pool, but long, narrow and winding. They were also caught in a strong current and moving forwards without having to kick their legs. Surrounding them were doughnut-shaped rings in different sizes, floating in the same direction.

"This must be the lazy river! Remember we added one to the drawing?" said Cassandra. "Quick, grab a ring. I'll show you how to get in." She ducked under the water and swam to the middle of the nearest doughnut. Up popped her head, then she hoisted herself up with her arms, flopped belly first over the side, and twisted around so her bottom was through the hole and her legs dangled over the edge. "The river looks cool from up here. Come on!"

Katy and Zia followed her lead, reaching for the doughnuts closest to them and trying their best to climb aboard. Zia succeeded after her third attempt, but Katy was struggling while holding onto a grumpy-looking Thunder, who kept accidentally puncturing doughnuts with his claws.

"I can't do it!" Katy cried in frustration. "Thunder, you've got to stop using your claws!"

"I knew this was a bad idea," Thunder replied crossly, as another doughnut started to deflate.

"Don't give up, guys. It's what you always say to me! Wait just a second and I'll come and help," offered Cassandra.

Cassandra had to use all her strength to fight against the current, but eventually she managed to paddle her doughnut alongside Katy, where she heaved a sulky Thunder onto her lap, careful to keep his claws away from the rubber ring, and held Katy's doughnut steady with her foot.

Katy, now free to use both her arms, finally clambered on, flopping herself back onto the ring with a sigh of relief. Then Cassandra caught a fourth, smaller ring with her foot and very gently – "No claws, remember!" – positioned an irritable Thunder inside.

29

Finally, all four members of the Playdate Adventure Club floated forwards, the backs of their heads resting comfortably on their rings as they gazed up at the cornflower blue sky. Katy's bedroom seemed a million miles away and at last they were all very much enjoying the ride.

CHAPTER FOUR

The journey downriver was so peaceful that Katy's eyes felt heavy. She guessed it was only a matter of time before she drifted off to sleep. The air was cool, the breeze was gently tickling her cheeks and the birds were singing in a cheerful chorus. Thunder was curled comfortably in his own ring, purring happily, clearly delighted to be out of the water at last. Katy's best friends were floating along by her side while sunshine glimmered on the surface of the water. It was pure heaven.

But Katy was tugged from her dreamy state when she caught sight of their surroundings. On either side of them, they were drifting past rooftops. "Guys, look!" she gasped. "Over there!"

"Our school!" Zia exclaimed, looking down as they floated past a rectangular building with colourful panels on the walls and a playground with hopscotch chalked onto the concrete. "What's our school doing here?"

"A lazy river in the sky. That's so cool!" Cassandra cried excitedly.

"I wonder what our class would say if they could see us now?" mused Katy.

"They wouldn't believe us," said Cassandra. "I don't think anyone would."

"Probably not," said Zia, "but we'll ace our ocean topic after this."

"If we ever get there!" Cassandra sighed.

Cassandra was right. They'd been floating

for ages now and, even though the river was relaxing, they should be getting on with their adventure. The thing was, there didn't seem to be any sign of the ocean, or an obvious way out of the lazy river.

"Any idea how we get back on the slide?" Zia asked.

They looked from one side of the river to the other, eyes peeled for an opening of some kind. And that's when they noticed the water up ahead behaving strangely – a bit like water in a bathtub just before it goes down a plughole. The current was pulling them along more forcefully now, then it sent them spinning unexpectedly round and round in a spiral.

Katy watched as Cassandra's, Zia's and Thunder's doughnuts suddenly flipped over, capsizing them into the water. Seconds later, Katy's ring also flew out from under her. She held

her breath and managed to grab hold of
Thunder just before she was dragged under.

She could feel her feet being sucked through
an opening beneath her, followed by her legs,
her tummy, her arms and shoulders, her head
and...

PLOP!

She landed
back on the
slide, Thunder
in her arms.

Immediately,
they were caught
up in the thrill

36

of the ride again, picking up speed as they slid over and under, round and round, up and down. Sometimes the slide was completely covered, like a tunnel, and they couldn't see where they were. Other times, there was a clear panel, like a window to the world, and the outside rushed past them – cities, mountains, lakes and rivers – in a colourful blur. There were flashing lights and jets of water shooting from the ceiling, and music pulsing all around them. Then, at last, just as before when they'd been fired with a pop straight into the lazy river, Katy was suddenly – and unexpectedly – plunged into cold, salty water.

The force of the impact made her lose her hold on Thunder as she was submerged. She kicked her legs as hard as she could and used her arms to try to swim up. Waves were rolling above her, but even trying with all her might Katy knew she wasn't going to break the surface before she would need to take in a gulp of air.

She kicked and kicked and pulled and pulled. She almost made it. But then her mouth opened and…just as she was expecting her lungs to fill with water, she found them inflating and deflating as normal. She could breathe underwater. The magic had worked!

She blinked a few times to allow her eyes to adjust, then looked around to check that Thunder and her friends were also OK. But

Cassandra and Zia were both shrieking and laughing – WOAH, they could laugh and talk underwater *as well*! – and were already doing underwater acrobatics in celebration of their new powers. Even Thunder seemed to be enjoying the water, kitty-paddling in circles with his one blue eye twinkling mischievously and a wide grin across his face.

"I have to admit," he said, "water isn't all bad."

Katy giggled. "I knew you'd love it once we got here!"

"Well, I wouldn't go that far," he smirked.

"Hey, I feel like a mermaid!" shouted Cassandra.

"And me!" Katy cried as her long ponytail fanned out behind her. She'd never been a confident swimmer and had ALWAYS struggled to master the dolphin kick, but now it felt like the most natural thing in the world.

"Watch me!" Zia shouted, somersaulting forwards and backwards, backwards and forwards. "It's so easy! I feel like a mermaid as well!"

"You look like one too!" Katy joked. "Your plait's out of control!"

Everyone joined in the fun, twisting and gliding through the water as if in slow motion. Even Thunder, who they joked was like a *purr*-maid, managed a roly-poly with his long grey tail tucked between his legs.

40

At last they stopped to catch their breath and looked around once more. Way above, sunlight was streaming through the surface of the ocean in thin rays, making the water twinkle like tiny diamonds. Surrounding them was never-ending water as far as the eye could see and beneath them was...

"What's that?" yelped Katy, as something huge and dark loomed up from below.

"Let's check it out!" Zia replied excitedly, always the explorer.

"If you say so," Cassandra muttered, trying to appear more confident than she felt.

Cautiously, they swam a little closer, and that's when they saw it – a magnificent shipwreck lying motionless on the seabed. It looked like it had been frozen in time for hundreds of years.

CHAPTER FIVE

"Careful, Zia. You don't know what could be hiding inside," Cassandra warned, as they swam in single file alongside a porthole, Zia way out in front.

"I will be, I promise!" Zia smiled back at them. "I've just ALWAYS wanted to see a shipwreck. Doesn't it make you think of pirates and treasure?"

"And danger!" Cassandra replied.

"Good point. But I still think we should look inside. If I promise to go carefully."

Zia looked at them pleadingly with wide eyes.

The shipwreck had once been a beautiful wooden pirate ship. It looked like one you'd find in a storybook, with a long prow, now worn and splintered, and two jagged stumps where the tall masts once stood. It was split right down the middle, with the bow and stern lying a few metres apart, the bow toppled over to one side. The hull was battered and slime covered, and the crow's nest, which would once have been a vital lookout point for navigating the high seas, lay smashed to pieces, home to tiny barnacles and cream-coloured limpets.

"I have to admit, it's pretty incredible," said Katy.

"Only pretty incredible? Don't you mean ABSOLUTELY AMAZINGLY incredible?" Zia squealed with delight.

"Obviously that's what I mean!" Katy winked at her. "Come on, I can't see any sharks or anything. Let's look inside."

The girls swam through the gap between the bow and the stern and could now see clearly that the ship had an upper and lower deck. Its enormous steering wheel was propped up on its side with one of the splintered spokes caught part way through a porthole. The decks themselves were also weathered and broken.

"It's sad, don't you think?" said Cassandra thoughtfully.

"What do you mean, sad?" Zia asked.

"That this has been lying here for hundreds of years. Doesn't it make you wonder why it sank?"

"I just keep thinking about all the juicy mice that would have once lived on board!" Thunder exclaimed.

"You would be thinking about that, wouldn't you?" Katy giggled, ruffling his fur, which wasn't so easy to do underwater.

Zia let out an almighty shriek and everyone jumped out of their skin.

"W-w-what is it? W-w-what have you seen?" Cassandra sounded panicked.

"It's a treasure chest! Quick, over here!"

The others swam over to where Zia was wrestling with the lid of a huge box.

"Imagine if it's full of gold and jewels!" Zia said dreamily. "Help me with this lid, will you?"

Six hands and two front paws pulled and prised and tried their hardest to loosen the lid, but still it refused to budge. Finally, when they'd almost given up hope, the lid suddenly sprang open.

They gasped in shock as a small school of orange and black stripy clownfish darted past them, as if desperate to get away. Once they'd all gone, the girls took a deep breath and peered inside.

"Nothing!" Thunder frowned. "Absolutely nothing!"

"Never mind. Mum always says the excitement's in the looking," said Zia, but Katy could tell she was disappointed.

"Come on, let's go," she said, touching Zia gently on the shoulder. "Perhaps it's time for

47

us to be getting on with our ocean adventure anyway, hey?"

"You're right. And we might even come across another shipwreck," said Zia hopefully. "Did you know there are at least three million of them in the oceans?" Zia always knew lots of interesting facts.

They all turned and swam back through the gap into the wide, open sea, searching for where their adventure would take them next. But, one by one, the girls noticed something very strange. The fish in the treasure chest were the only other creatures they'd seen so far on their adventure.

They'd imagined the world underwater to be brimming with colour and teeming with life, with rainbow corals and shoals of multicoloured fish and sparkling sea anemones and all sorts of other incredible creatures. As they continued to swim, however, the girls could only spot a few lone fish in the distance. It was hard to see clearly as the water was dark and dingy away from the surface. But when they looked harder at what the fish were doing, it seemed every one of them was swimming in the same direction – and that was away from the girls.

"What do you think's wrong with the fish?" asked Cassandra. "Have we disturbed them?"

"Maybe they're scared I'm going to eat them!" Thunder laughed.

"Thunder! You wouldn't? You can't!" said Katy. "It wouldn't be right!"

"I'm joking." He winked. "You know I'm more of a mouse cat myself."

But Katy had stopped listening to Thunder's poor taste in humour. She was busy studying something small and orange caught on the straps of her swimsuit. "Look at this!" she tutted, picking the orange thing off and holding it out in front to show her friends. "It's part of a crisp packet. Look – there are tiny bits of plastic everywhere!"

When they'd been studying the ocean at school, Ms Coco had told them about the amount of plastic in the sea. They'd seen a film about it in class – how so much plastic is used and wasted across the world that it can end up washing into rivers and oceans. Katy remembered how the whole class had almost cried when they saw a seal struggling with a ribbon of plastic caught around its neck. But not even the film could have prepared them for seeing all this plastic in the ocean for real.

"It's horrible!" Zia snivelled, as a shoal of fish swam past, this time chased by a plastic bottle. There were more fish now, but they were still clearly swimming away from the girls.

"It's like the slide has dumped us in the middle of a rubbish tip!" cried Cassandra.

A dolphin then swam up alongside the girls, staring at them with kind and knowing eyes. Katy had always adored dolphins – she loved how smiley they always looked. Apart from cats and horses, they were her absolute favourite animals. The dolphin looked straight at the girls, then tilted its head and nodded its nose in the direction of the shoals of fish.

"Do you think it's asking us to follow?" Cassandra asked.

"I'm not sure. But I think we should – I'd love to know where the fish are going," said Zia, already swimming on ahead.

"Anything to get away from all this plastic!" Thunder mumbled, paddling his paws hard alongside Katy and Cassandra as they swam to catch up with their eager friend.

Butterflies had reappeared in Katy's tummy and were busy flapping their tiny little wings. She didn't know where the dolphin was taking them, but she felt sure they were about to be shown something completely unexpected.

CHAPTER SIX

The dolphin was a fast swimmer – almost as fast as the orca had been during their North Pole adventure. The friends swam as hard as they could to catch up with it, with Katy holding onto Thunder's paw so he didn't get left behind. They saw an enormous stingray flying gracefully through the water, a glossy black eel with sharp teeth and a mean face, and two tiny yellow sea horses no bigger than their hands. Little bits of plastic were still bobbing around them, caught in the ocean currents.

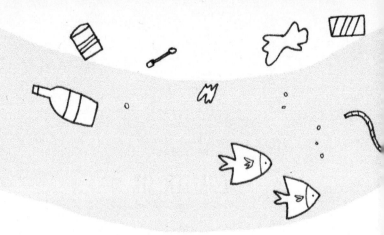

When they were finally level with the dolphin and kicking their feet in rhythm with its tail, the dolphin stopped, turned and spoke.

"Do you know where the fish are going?" it asked.

The girls shook their heads, trying hard to catch their breath.

"Can you see anything wrong with the water we're swimming in?"

"You mean the plastic?" said Cassandra. "Yes, and it's terrible."

The dolphin nodded. "There is a legendary cave in the middle of the Atlantic Ocean, as beautiful and clean as any cave you'll ever find."

The dolphin sighed. "It's where sea life can go for protection when the world they live in is no longer safe. Now the ocean is so full of plastic, all the creatures you see are fleeing their homes in search of this cave. They want to live in a place that is clean and safe again."

The girls lowered their heads. The plastic was everywhere and they understood why the fish were trying to find somewhere else to live. But even worse was the fact that humans were to blame – just as they were to blame for the litter on the streets back home and the melting polar ice caps. They'd seen destruction caused by humans on previous adventures. Now, even surrounded by cool seawater, they could feel their cheeks burning in shame.

"We're sorry," Katy said quietly. "It must be awful to have to flee your home."

"Humans do some terrible things." Thunder

nodded and Katy eyed him anxiously. "But you can trust these girls," he continued, looking seriously at the dolphin with his one eye. "They'd do anything to help."

"He's right." Zia smiled. "We'd do anything."

"Anything!" Cassandra echoed, while Katy squeezed her friends' hands.

The dolphin thought for a moment. "Do you really mean it? I have an important job to do before getting to the cave. Will you come with me?"

"We will," the girls said in unison, nodding eagerly.

"If you need help, Thunder's your cat!" said Thunder, flexing his small cat muscles.

They all laughed.

"I'm Lana by the way," said the dolphin, smiling for the first time since they'd met. "It means 'calm as still water'. It's nice to meet you all. Now, please, we don't have much time. Follow me."

And she was off again, flicking her tail and gliding smoothly through the ocean in the direction of the other sea creatures. They passed more shoals of coloured fish, a blue jellyfish with a pink crown and long blue tentacles, a starfish with  bright orange arms and a mother turtle swimming with a string of baby turtles in her wake.

Katy was certain she also saw a shark in the distance, with a head shaped like a hammer. She moved closer to her friends – there was safety in numbers.

"Where do you think we're going?" Cassandra whispered. They were lagging behind Lana now, trying to keep up – although Cassandra was finding the swimming easier than the others.

"No idea. But Lana seems pretty worried about whatever it is," Zia whispered back.

"I guess we just have to trust her," said Katy, pushing herself harder, all the time holding on tightly to Thunder's paw.

"Yes, we can't back out now. Come on!" Cassandra encouraged them.

Suddenly, Lana darted left, leaving the mass of sea creatures and swimming out into clearer water. "We're almost there," she shouted back to the girls, nodding her nose to show them the way, before diving deeper towards the ocean floor.

"Goodness! She doesn't give us much time to rest!" Zia puffed, lowering her head so she could follow Lana in a dive. "I'm exhausted already."

But just as Katy was about to respond, she saw something below that made her stomach squirm. Lying on the seabed was a purple octopus, fighting to free its arms from something trapping them against its body. It looked like it was crying.

At once, they knew why Lana had brought them here.

CHAPTER SEVEN

True to her name, Lana spoke calmly to the octopus. "Shh, now, we're here to help," she said, "but you need to stop struggling. When you struggle, the plastic tightens and tangles even more."

The octopus cried louder and continued to thrash about. Thin nylon rope was tied in knots around it, cutting into its skin, and it was trying desperately to escape.

"Shh, you must stay still," said Lana softly. "I promise we can set you free."

Finally, the octopus stopped moving and allowed its eight arms to go limp. Immediately, Lana got to work, pulling at the rope with her nose and biting it with her teeth.

Katy and the others didn't waste a second either. They rushed to the octopus's side, tugging at the knots with fingers and claws and trying to pull each of the eight arms free. It was harder than it looked – the rope was in a complete tangle and wound so tightly around the octopus's body. They had to be patient and use sheer determination.

It was only when Thunder started chewing through the rope that it began to break and become loose. Slowly, one by one, the octopus's arms were released until all that remained was the last bit of string tied around its middle. With one final pull from everyone, the octopus was free.

At once, it shot up through the water, spinning round and round in celebration of its new-found freedom. The octopus wiggled its eight arms to make certain no lasting damage was done, then it called down to the small team of rescuers below.

"I don't know how to thank you!" the octopus exclaimed. "I was on my way to the cave to get away from the plastic. Then I swam straight into this rope and the current wrapped it around me. Every time I tried to break free, I found myself tangled even more."

"No need to thank us," Lana called back. "You're one of the lucky ones. Now go!"

And just like that, the octopus was off, wriggling its arms to propel itself through the water, where it soon joined the other sea creatures swimming in a constant stream above them.

"Good job, everyone," said Lana gratefully. "Especially you, Thunder."

The girls put their arms around the cat. Thunder, of course, lapped up all the attention.

"But we need to get going," the dolphin continued. "There are other creatures who need our help."

"How many?" Zia asked.

Lana shook her head sadly. "Too many, I'm afraid. That's why we can't afford to delay."

She swam away hurriedly, flicking her tail as she sped through the water, and the girls and Thunder followed. But their adventure felt different now. The thrills of the magical slide seemed a lifetime ago. They'd had no idea when they set off that their ocean adventure would become so important.

For the next hour they continued with their rescue mission. They saved a small parrot fish trapped inside the finger of a clear plastic glove, a massive turtle who had a plastic bag stuck in its throat and a baby whale caught in a broken fishing net.

Eventually, Lana turned to them and spoke. "The ocean is huge and we've only covered a small area today. Just think how many other creatures are trapped in a similar way. We don't have time to save them all."

The girls nodded. Even though they'd been told about it back home, none of them had really understood how much the plastic in the ocean was harming the creatures that lived there.

"So, this cave you spoke about," said Katy curiously. "It's actually real, then? I mean, all the creatures seem to know where they're going."

"Yes," Lana answered. "The legend turned out to be true. There is a cave and it's more wonderful than you could possibly imagine. Come, let's go and see it."

Joining the migration of sea creatures was like joining in a conga line. There were big fish, little fish, mammals, crustaceans, all swimming together, hoping to find a better place to live.

They'd been swimming for a while when suddenly the sea creatures came to a stop. The girls almost crashed into the back of a small seal pup in front of them and felt their feet pricked by the point of a swordfish's snout.

"Why have we stopped?" asked Cassandra.

"Thank goodness we have!" whispered Zia, out of breath.

"The cave is big," Lana explained, "but there's a queue to get in. We must enter one by one."

They shunted forwards slowly, until at last they could see the cave entrance. There was a dolphin at the front of the long line, holding a sort of clipboard made out of fastened-together razor shells. It was carving marks on it with a piece of sharp coral as it questioned each creature entering the cave.

"What is your species? Where are you from?"

the dolphin asked wearily, when the girls made it to the front. Then it looked up from the razor-clam clipboard and stared at Thunder and the girls with a puzzled expression on its face. Clearly, they weren't the kind of creatures it had expected to see.

"They're with me," said Lana, smiling. "And they won't be staying. They helped with my rescue mission today and are here to see the cave."

The other dolphin nodded, letting them through.

"Here we go," said Katy, briefly squeezing her friends' hands before releasing them to swim through the rocky opening.

"There's no going back now," Zia whispered, following her.

The walls were thick, the tunnel dark and they could just about make out a small sliver of light far ahead. They swam towards it and

71

when they finally emerged from the darkness, what opened in front of them was beyond even their wildest dreams.

CHAPTER EIGHT

The sides and floor of the cave were decorated with corals in an array of brilliant colours. There were fields of sea grasses, patches of pristine white sand and rays of sunlight streaming through gaps above them, casting everything in a magical, shimmering glow. All around the friends, the cave was teeming with life. There were fish of every shape and colour, eels and turtles and octopuses and squid and crabs and lobsters and porpoises and sharks and whales, and other creatures they couldn't even name.

73

And there wasn't any plastic –
not one piece of it anywhere!
The water was bright turquoise
and crystal clear.

But there was a problem.

The queue to get into the cave was so long that, when Katy had entered with her friends, she couldn't see the end of it behind them. But the cave was bursting with life and seemed completely full. Katy didn't see how the creatures lining up outside would ever fit in.

"Lana, what happens when there isn't any space left inside for the creatures outside?" she asked.

"I've been wondering the same thing," said Cassandra, nervously tugging at her curls.

"Is there another cave next door or something?" asked Zia.

Lana shook her head. "I'm afraid this is the only one. And you're right, there isn't room for everyone."

"So what happens to the other creatures?" asked Katy.

"Where do they go?" asked Cassandra.

75

"I'm afraid they must be left to find their own path."

"Even with all that plastic around them?" asked Thunder, horrified.

"Even then," said Lana. "I'm sorry." Then she turned and swam away to join in a conversation with a group of humpback whales.

The girls didn't like Lana's answer. There had to be another way. Surely there was something they could do?

"We need to come up with a plan," Cassandra said urgently, turning to Katy and Zia. "We can't go home when we know there are still animals in danger. It wouldn't be right."

"Hey, where's Thunder?" Katy asked, realising her cat

wasn't with them. They looked around until Zia spotted him close by, poking at a patch of sea anemones, their tentacles disappearing inside their jelly-like bodies as he swiped at them with his paw.

"Thunder, can you come over here?" Katy called out above the noise of the cave. "We've got something important to talk to you about."

But as she watched the sea anemones' tentacles appear then disappear again, an idea began to form in her mind. It started as a small seed in the deepest part of her brain, then gradually began to grow and take shape. She didn't know if it would work. She'd see

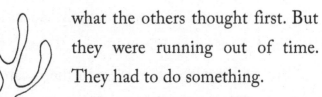

what the others thought first. But they were running out of time. They had to do something.

"Are you OK?" asked Cassandra.

Katy realised she must have been staring blankly into space while she'd been thinking. "Yes, sorry," she said, turning to face her friends. "Those sea anemones, they've given me an idea."

 Katy saw Thunder swipe his paw one more time at the mischievous creatures, then he paddled over to join the girls.

"I almost had that one," he said, licking his paw. "So, what do you want to discuss?"

"We need to make the plastic disappear," Katy announced.

"Well, yeah, but how?" asked Cassandra.

"It's like when the sea anemones suck in their tentacles – we need something that does the same to the plastic. Something that sucks it up, like a giant ocean hoover!"

"But nothing like that exists in the ocean," grumbled Thunder.

"Thunder's right, Katy," Zia agreed. "Where are we going to find a thing like that?"

Just then, Cassandra's eyes lit up – she'd figured out where Katy was going with her plan. "You mean, where could we possibly find a big tube that opens right into the ocean?"

Zia and Thunder continued to stare with blank looks on their faces.

"A big tube with magical powers?" Katy added.

Suddenly the penny dropped.

"THE SLIDE!" they chanted.

"EXACTLY!" shouted Katy. "If we can somehow reverse the magic, so the slide sucks things into it rather than shooting things out of it, we could use it for the greatest ocean clean-up mission of all time!"

"Katy, you're a genius!" said Cassandra, throwing her arms around her friend's shoulders.

Zia didn't look quite so convinced. "Have you

thought about where the plastic is going to go?" she asked. "If it's sucked up by the slide, isn't it all going to end up in your bedroom?"

"I'd wondered about that," said Katy worriedly. "Any ideas?"

They were silent for a moment, as they all wracked their brains.

Then: "I've got it!" Cassandra blurted out. "Haven't you always wondered what the lazy river was for?"

Now it was Katy's turn to frown.

"That's it!" shouted Zia. "Surely the river is big enough to contain the plastic. I know rivers usually lead to the sea, but this one doesn't. It just goes round and round in a continuous winding loop. It's like one great big, magical storage tank!"

It's what Katy loved most about her friends. Each of their brains worked differently so that, by joining their ideas together, they always came up with the very best solutions.

Once they'd put the finishing touches to their plan and were sure they knew exactly how it would work, they called Lana over to explain.

"Do you really think it could work?" asked the dolphin doubtfully.

"We can't say for certain," said Katy. "But isn't it worse if we don't try? You see, when the four of us joined hands in my bedroom, the magic we produced was big enough to create a waterslide that brought us here and gave us the power to breathe underwater. Think what could happen if every creature here joined together. If we all concentrate our hardest and imagine the slide sucking up the plastic, I'm sure we can succeed!"

Lana still looked uneasy, but she called the creatures in the cave to gather round and

81

explained the rather unusual plan to them. When she'd finished, Katy addressed the hushed crowds.

"For this to work, we all need to link together – your fins, tails, claws, arms, shells or tentacles." Katy waited until the creatures had rearranged themselves around the cave in a big spaghetti-like circuit. "Now, close your eyes and imagine the slide turning into one giant suction device," she continued.

"Imagine it sucking up every last morsel of plastic in the ocean. Imagine all this plastic rushing up through the tube, straight into a magical river hovering above us in the sky. Channel all your energy into this image. Then repeat after me: I wish for a plastic-free ocean."

"*I wish for a plastic-free ocean*," the creatures chorused.

At once, the cave began to rumble. Katy, Zia, Cassandra, Thunder and Lana broke their holds and swam as fast as they could back through the tunnel to see what was happening in the ocean.

They were just in time. Little bits of plastic floating in the sea around them were vibrating faster and faster, until suddenly they began shooting through the water, whizzing away in the direction of the slide. Katy had to dive out of the path of an oncoming bottle zooming at speed and Lana only just managed to avoid a plastic bag getting caught on her fin.

CHAPTER NINE

The friends watched, stunned, as the ocean slowly changed before their eyes. The water was becoming clearer, turning from murky green to sparkling turquoise. The long queue of creatures lining up at the cave entrance, so quiet and sombre moments before, were now loud and full of cheer, ducking out of the way of the plastic and looking around in disbelief. Could this really be happening? Was all the plastic finally disappearing?

"It's working!" exclaimed Zia, trying not to

sound too surprised.

"You did it, Katy!" said Cassandra.

"We did it, you mean!" Katy threw her arms around her friends and hugged them close. "I may have had the idea, but it wouldn't have happened without your help."

Katy felt a cold nose nudging against her shin.

"And yours, Thunder. No adventure would be complete without you by our side."

"You've saved us. I don't know how to thank you." Lana smiled as the entrance to the cave split open in a loud CRACK and all the creatures inside burst out. The dolphins were doing somersaults, the fish were darting around in great shimmering shoals, the octopuses were spinning like ballerinas and the crustaceans were clicking their pincers and claws in delight. It was a circus performance that went on...

and on…and on…as creature after creature continued to pour out of the cave.

"Your slide really is magical!" gasped Lana, when the last creature had finally swum away, back to its clean home.

"It's amazing what you can achieve if you wish strongly enough," said Katy, as she held onto her friends' hands.

"It's what makes our adventures special," added Cassandra.

"But we never thought we'd be leading the greatest ocean clean-up mission of all time!" Katy laughed.

"All because you used your hearts and your heads." Lana bowed in honour of what they'd done. "That's a true gift. You should feel proud."

The girls beamed, thrilled to have been able to help.

"Before you go, I have something for you," Lana said. "Wait here just a second." She disappeared briefly into the cave, then swam back with something in her mouth. She dropped a small, hard object first into Katy's hands, then Zia's and Cassandra's, and finally into Thunder's paws. "A token to remember us by."

Katy opened her fingers a fraction, just enough to see a tiny blue dolphin crafted from little pieces of shell resting on her palm. She had to clasp her fist tightly to stop it from floating away. But Thunder's paws were better at swiping at objects than holding them, and his dolphin danced around in the ocean's current as he tried to catch it.

"Here, I'll look after it!" Katy giggled, rescuing the little dolphin before pulling Thunder in with her free arm. "And I think it's time we got you back on dry land!" She laughed.

"Lana, we're really going to miss you," said Cassandra. "But we need to go home now too."

They said their goodbyes to Lana, thanking her for their gifts and hugging her velvety smooth body. Then they moved to form a circle, Thunder in the middle, and closed their eyes.

"*I wish to go home,*" they said in unison.

Katy imagined her bedroom back home, a warm breeze blowing through the open window, her dad making dinner in the kitchen across the hall.

At once, the girls started to feel hot and cold and bubbly. Their bodies were filled with electric currents, shooting around their insides from the tops of their heads to the tips of their toes. Only when it all stopped did they open their eyes.

89

They were standing in Katy's bedroom, next to the window, the heat of the day just beginning to fade. Thunder was cleaning behind his ears, having returned to his normal cat-self, and Katy felt the relief of being surrounded by warm and sticky air rather than chilly, wet saltwater. It felt so natural standing on solid ground that it was easy to doubt whether they'd been on an ocean adventure at all! But Katy swore she could see a small piece of seaweed caught on one of Cassandra's hair clips.

"Hey!" cried Cassandra. "The dolphin – it's another charm!" She beamed with excitement.

"Come on, let's add them to the others," Zia said, opening her hand with a smile.

On previous adventures they'd been given a star and a snowflake, which they'd attached to a bracelet they each wore to remind them of their magical playdates. The tiny blue dolphin made the perfect addition and Thunder's charm looked smart hanging from his collar.

"Did that really just happen?" said Cassandra, blinking, as Zia helped her secure the dolphin onto her wrist. "Did we really just clean up the ocean?"

"Oh, I hope so," said Zia wishfully. "Although, even if we have, I don't know how long it will stay clean for."

"We have to keep trying to do our bit," said Katy. "Use less plastic, for starters. Maybe we could do a class presentation on it, like the one we did about the North Pole?"

The others nodded.

"Where to next, then? Cassie, it has to be your turn to host the next playdate adventure. You get to choose again," said Zia.

Thunder glanced up from licking his paw and stared at them pleadingly with his one blue eye.

"OK, I promise it won't be a water adventure

this time!" Cassandra giggled. "Somewhere more cat friendly. In fact, there will be plenty of birds and squirrels to chase!"

Katy could hear her dad calling them for dinner. But just as she turned to leave her bedroom, something made her stop and glance back through the open window. The clouds were moving strangely through the sky. They'd formed a pattern that looked very much like a river winding its way over the rooftops.

"Look!" she shouted. "Look at the clouds!"

Cassandra and Zia turned, but the clouds had already parted and floated away. Maybe Katy had imagined it, or maybe there really was a magical river somewhere in the sky.

How to Plan Your Own
Playdate Adventure

1. Decide where you would like to go on your adventure.

2. Plan how you would get there. Do you need to build anything or imagine yourself in a new land?

3. Imagine what exciting or challenging things might happen on your adventure.

4. Decide if you are going to learn anything from your adventure.

5. Most important of all, remember to have fun!

THE OCEAN

Did you know…?

Oceans cover more than 70%
of the Earth's surface.

An incredible 94% of all living species
exist in the ocean.

Around 70% of the oxygen we breathe is
produced by the ocean.

On average, eight million tonnes of plastic end
up in our oceans every year, either as larger,
recognisable items such as plastic bags and
fishing nets, or microplastics, which are tiny
pieces of plastic smaller than your fingernail.

Around 90% of sea birds and fish are believed to have plastic particles in their stomachs.

The UN estimates plastic is killing around one million seabirds and 100,000 sea creatures every year.

People are not going to stop making or using plastic. It is cheap to produce and hard-wearing, which makes it useful. But there are things we can all do to reduce the amount of plastic pollution:

- Practise the three "Rs" – reduce the amount of plastic you use, reuse plastic when you can and recycle as much of your plastic as possible.
- Drink water from reusable bottles.
- Reuse carrier bags when you go shopping.
- Join, or start, a plastic clean-up group. If you live near the seaside, there are "beach clean-up days" you could get involved with.
- Educate yourselves on what can and can't be recycled in your area, learn about the problems with plastic pollution and talk about it with friends and family.

Emma Beswetherick is the mother of two young children and wanted to write exciting, inspirational and enabling adventure stories to share with her daughter. Emma is a publisher with Little, Brown and lives in south-west London with her family and two ragdoll cats, one of whom was the inspiration for Thunder. *The Magic Ocean Slide* is her third book.

Anna Woodbine is an independent book designer and illustrator based in the hills near Bath. She works on all sorts of book covers from children's to adult's, classics to crime, memoirs to meditation. She takes her tea with a dash of milk (Earl Grey, always), loves the wind in her face, comfortable shoes and that lovely damp smell after it's rained.

Find her at: thewoodbineworkshop.co.uk

JOIN THE CONVERSATION ONLINE!

Follow us for a behind-the-scenes
look at our books. There'll be exclusive
content and giveaways galore!
You can access learning resources here:
oneworld-publications.com/rtb
Find us on YouTube as
Oneworld Publications
on Facebook @oneworldpublications
and on Twitter @Rocktheboatnews